whose mouse are you?

BY ROBERT KRAUS • PICTURES BY JOSE ARUEGO

Aladdin Paperbacks
New York London Toronto Sydney

ALADDIN PAPERBACKS
An imprint of Simon & Schuster Children's Publishing Division
1230 Avenue of the Americas, New York, NY 10020

ALADDIN PAPERBACKS and colophon are registered trademarks of Simon & Schuster, Inc.
Also available in a Simon & Schuster Books for Young Readers hardcover edition.
Manufactured in China
First Aladdin Paperbacks edition 1986
Second Aladdin Paperbacks edition 1998
Third Aladdin Paperbacks edition June 2005
10 9 8 7 6 5 4

The Library of Congress has cataloged the hardcover edition as follows:
Kraus, Robert.
Whose mouse are you?
Reprint. Originally published; New York; Collier Books, 1972 c1970.
Summary: A lonely little mouse has to be resourceful in order to bring his family back together.
[1. Mice—Fiction. 2. Stories in rhyme]
I. Aruego, José   II. Title.
PZ8.3.K864Wh   1986   [E]   86-16376

ISBN 0-698-84052-7 (hc.)
ISBN 1-4169-0311-9 (pbk.)
1017 SCP

For Bruce and Billy

Whose mouse are you?

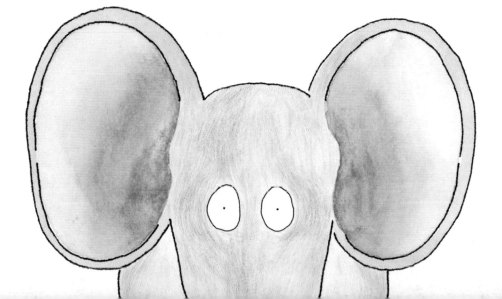

Nobody's mouse.

Where is your mother?

Inside the cat.

Where is your father?

Caught in a trap.

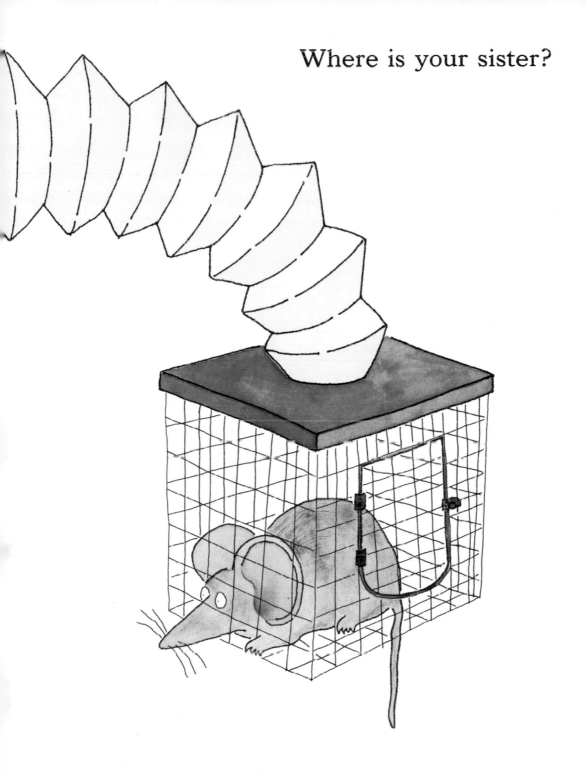

Where is your sister?

Far from home.

Where is your brother?

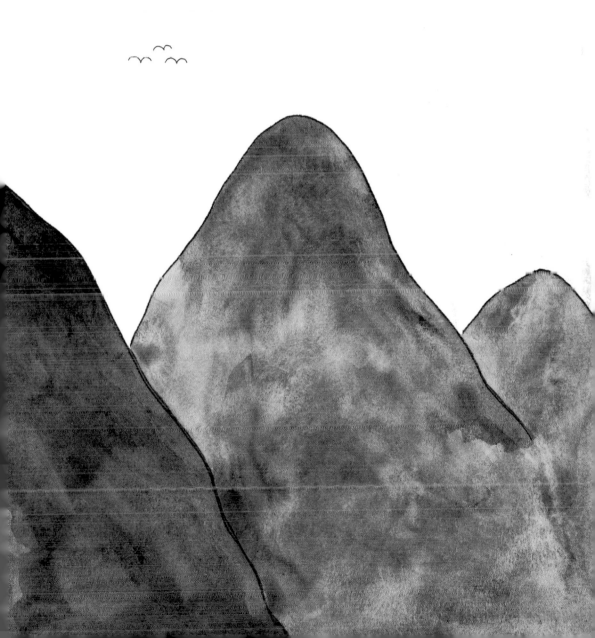

I have none.

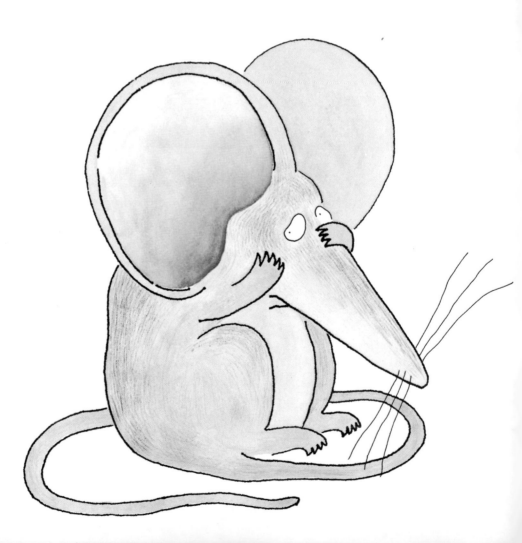

What will you do?

Shake my mother out of the cat!

Free my father from the trap!

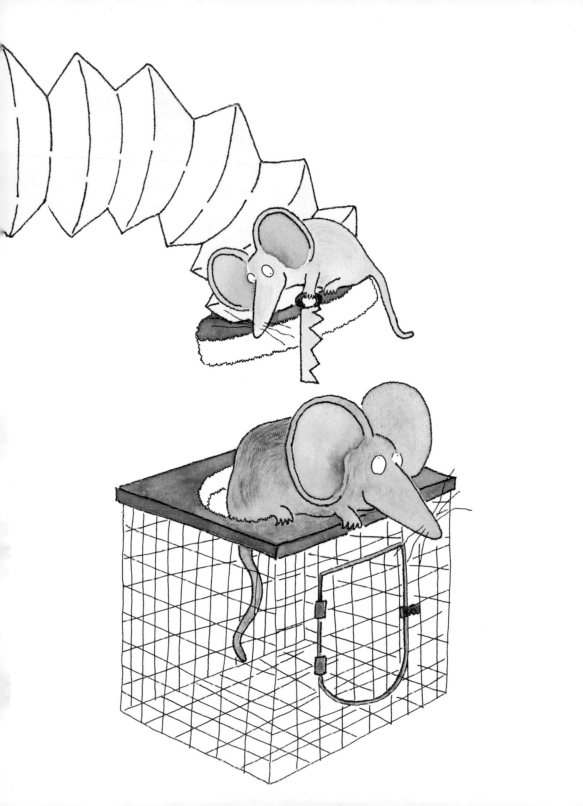

Find my sister and bring her home.

Wish for a brother as I have none.

Now whose mouse are you?

My mother's mouse, she loves me so.

My father's mouse, from head to toe.

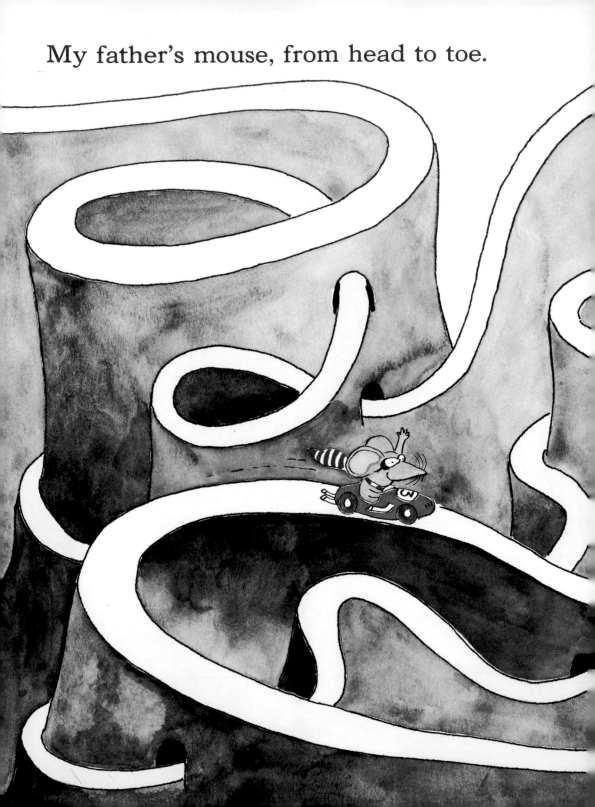

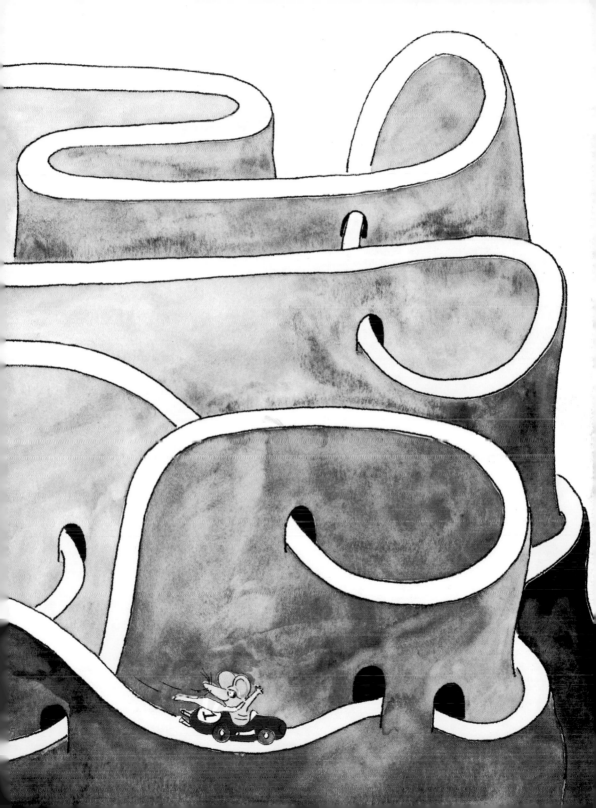

My sister's mouse, she loves me too.

My brother's mouse. . . .

Your brother's mouse?

My brother's mouse—he's *brand* new!